ANITA LOBEL

ONE LIGHTHOUSE, ONE MOON

Greenwillow Books
An Imprint of HarperCollinsPublishers

For Billy, who brought Nini home

Watercolor and gouache paints were used for the full-color art.
The text type is Adobe Catull.

One Lighthouse, One Moon
Copyright © 2000 by Anita Lobel
Printed in Singapore by Tien Wah Press. All rights reserved.
www.harperchildrens.com

Library of Congress Cataloging-in-Publication Data

Lobel, Anita.
One lighthouse, one moon / by Anita Lobel.
p.   cm.
"Greenwillow Books."
Summary: Presents the days of the week, the months of
the year, and numbers from one to ten through the
activities of a cat and people in and around a lighthouse.
ISBN 0-688-15539-1 (trade).
ISBN 0-688-15540-5 (lib. bdg.)
[1. Days–Fiction.   2. Months–Fiction.
3. Cats–Fiction.   4. Lighthouses–Fiction.
5. Counting.]   I. Title.   PZ7.L7794On
2000 [E]–dc21   98-50790   CIP   AC

2 3 4 5 6 7 8 9 10   First Edition

Contents

ALL WEEK LONG

MONDAY
TUESDAY
WEDNESDAY
THURSDAY
FRIDAY
SATURDAY
SUNDAY

Black shoes on MONDAY.

Red sh TUESDAY.

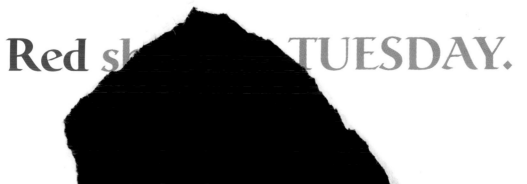

Blue shoes o~~n~~ ~~WED~~NESDAY.

Yellow shoes on THURSDAY.

Green shoes on FRIDAY.

Pink shoes on SATURDAY.

White shoes on **SUNDAY.**

**THE END
OF THE WEEK**

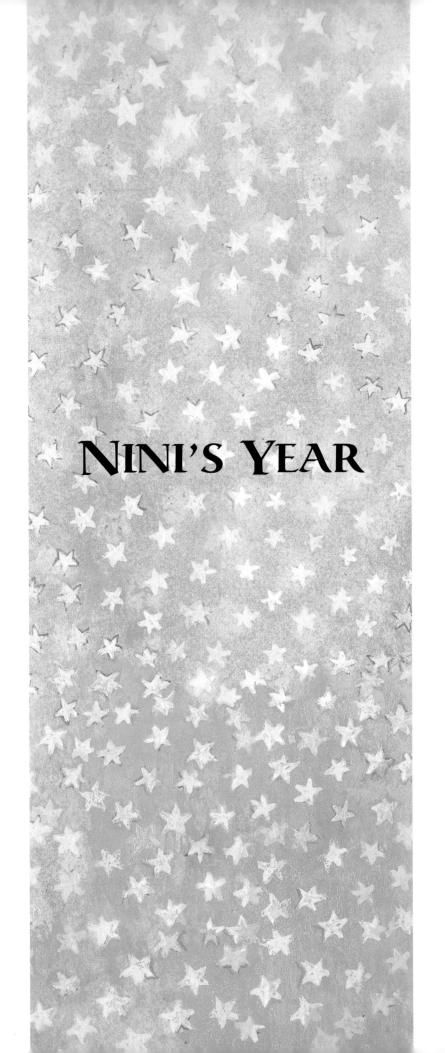

NINI'S YEAR

In JANUARY Nini caught
snowflakes on her nose.

In FEBRUARY Nini avoided
kisses on Valentine's Day.

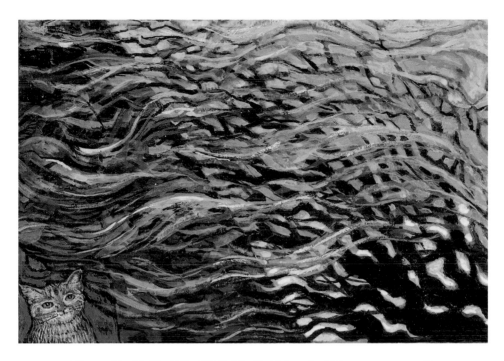

In MARCH Nini listened
to winds howling.

In APRIL Nini watched crocuses
poke through the ground.

In MAY Nini chased kites in the sky.

In JUNE Nini smelled roses
growing on a bush.

In JULY Nini napped under a flag.

In AUGUST Nini dreamed of crayfish.

In SEPTEMBER Nini played
in the autumn leaves.

In OCTOBER Nini posed on a pumpkin.

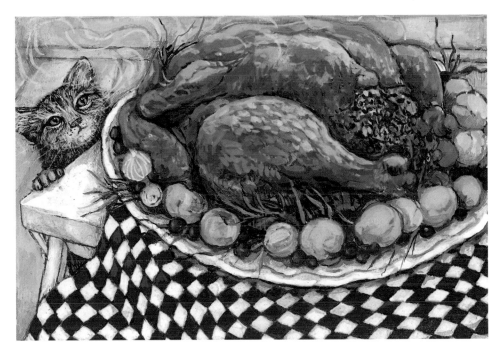

In NOVEMBER Nini smelled turkey.

In DECEMBER Nini waited for good things.

And they came.

THE END
OF THE YEAR

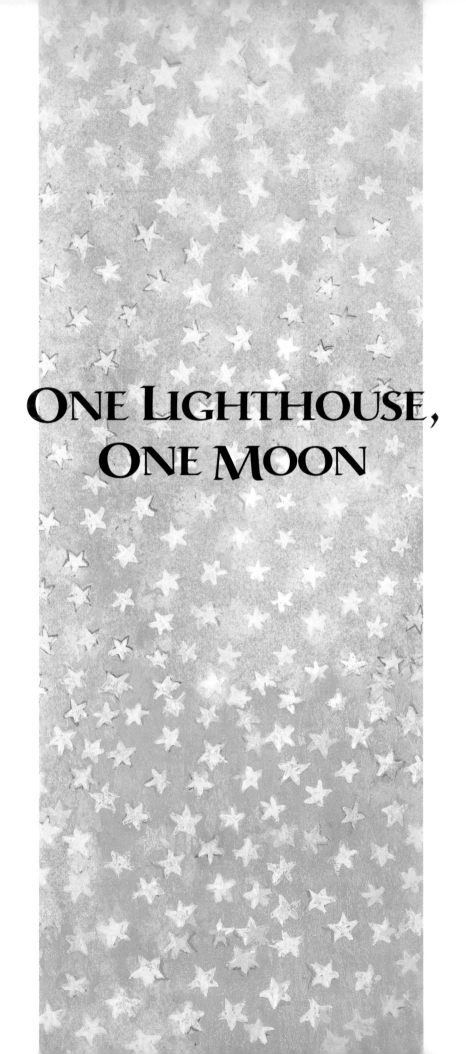

ONE LIGHTHOUSE,
ONE MOON

ONE lighthouse stood on a rock in the sea.

TWO boats sailed by.

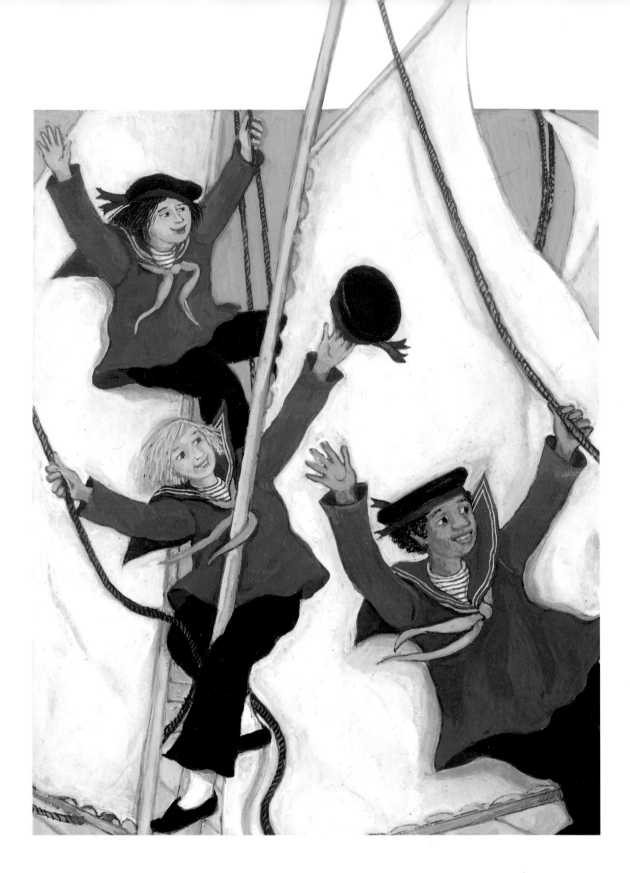

THREE sailors waved to

FOUR girls dancing
on the shore.

FIVE whales blew spouts
of water in the air.

SIX pelicans dozed.

SEVEN seagulls bobbed
on the waves.

EIGHT geese flew south
to avoid early snow.

NINE fisherfolk walked home with their catch.

TEN trees bent in the wind.

And ONE HUNDRED stars

and ONE moon lit up the sky.

**THE END
OF THE BOOK**